VOLUPTUOUS VERBS

SYNONYMS TO SPICE UP YOUR STEAMY SCENES

THESAURUS FOR ROMANCE WRITERS

LIZ ADAMS

VOLUPTUOUS VERBS
SYNONYMS TO SPICE UP YOUR STEAMY SCENES
THESAURUS FOR ROMANCE WRITERS

Published by: Writer's Fun Zone Publishing

ISBN-13: 978-1-944841-70-6

CONTENTS

PRAISE FOR LIZ ADAMS' FICTION

5 stars! Oh my, Alice!

"Alice in Wonderland is truly a one of a kind book to begin with, but to be able to completely rewrite it in a very adult fashion takes talent. The author sticks true to characters Alice meets in the original books but now all encounters are very sexual in nature. Love [Alice's Salacious Adventures: Lessons From Wonderland]! Can't wait to read the next book!"

—Nic & Kenzie C.

5 stars! This book has everything

"I really enjoyed [Alice's Story of O: The Princess and the Pea]. It was so well written and it is very good. I will definitely read this book over again and recommend it!!"

—Carol Albertson-Breckenridge

5 stars! Dived in

"First time reading [Liz Adams], and wow I was sucked in. Loved [de Sade & Grimm: A Steamy Collection of Dark Delights] and I want more. I highly recommend."

—munchkinbetty

5 stars! Liz Adams does it again

"[Sherlock: The Casebook of a Salacious Sleuth] is a book with four spicy stories all relating to Sherlock Holmes. They are fun and steamy and the cases are interesting in each. If you love erotica, Liz Adams is definitely someone you should be reading."

—Taryn Schilling

INTRODUCTION TO THE THESAURUS SERIES

This is a thesaurus series I wish I had when I started writing sex scenes. While writing about a coupling, I'd spend countless hours searching for synonyms. When I wrote historical spicy scenes, I spent even more time working out if the synonyms were relevant to the time period I was writing in.

I wrote this thesaurus series for myself so that, in one trilogy of books, I can find powerful verbs and adjectives to improve my writing, plus plenty of historically accurate nouns to give my stories a flavor of authenticity.

OVERVIEW OF HOW THIS SERIES IS ORGANIZED

This thesaurus series is divided into three main sections: verbs, adjectives, and historical nouns. One book for each.

Voluptuous Verbs (this book): The verbs are organized from early stages of desire to recovery from a sweaty bout of amorous aerobics.

Arousing Adjectives: The adjectives are organized describing the body from head to toe, and all of the excitement that happens along the journey.

Naughty Nouns: The nouns are organized by date of first popular use from head to toe, then to genitals; then from foreplay to the full snog.

A NOTE ABOUT LANGUAGE: MAKE NOTE OF YOUR PREFERENCES

At first glance, many of the verbs and adjectives may seem odd or misplaced. That's where your creativity comes in. For example, instead of writing, "She accommodated his entrance," you could write, "She negotiated his entrance." In context, the reader would understand the sentence.

A NOTE ABOUT HOW THE BOOKS ARE FORMATTED

I've formatted the print edition and the digital edition a little differently due to the benefit of each format.

If you have the print version of this book, I've left space beside the words in case you want to jot down your thoughts on a particular word, i.e., which ones would be great for explicit scenes, which would be great for subtle scenes, which would be great for the meet cute, etc. You can also note your favorite words in the "Personal Favorites" section at the end of the book.

If you have the digital version, you may be able to underline or highlight your favorite terms. Optionally, others with the ebook version might see which terms you (anonymously) <u>underlined</u>, and you might see the terms they underlined. In this way, you can receive real-time feedback on the words readers of this ebook like the most.

A NOTE ABOUT LANGUAGE - TRIGGER WARNING

WARNING: Many of the words are profane, and some are even insulting and violent. Don't read this book if profanity and violent terminology offends you. You have been warned!

Happy word hunting!

BUT WAIT! THERE'S MORE! - BONUS PRINTABLE WORKSHEET

Go to LizAdamsAuthor.com/thesaurus to download a handsome worksheet you can use to keep notes of your favorite verbs, adjectives, and historically accurate nouns.

WHO THIS THESAURUS SERIES IS FOR AND NOT FOR

WHO THIS SERIES IS FOR

The *Thesaurus for Romance Writers* series is not just for romance authors. This series is for any writer who has drafted a sex scene in their story and wants to be sure the quality of the scene matches the experience you're trying to convey.

If you want to convey a subtle, intimate connection between the characters, this book can help you find the language you need. Want to encourage the reader to experience an insatiable lust that requires hands-on reading? This thesaurus has just the words you're looking for.

Genres can include anything from spicy romance to paranormal tales, to thrillers, to sci-fi adventures, as long as there is at least one scene of sexual intimacy.

WHO THIS SERIES IS NOT FOR

This thesaurus is not for writers of sweet romance nor any genre that doesn't include any sex scenes. Also, profanity and naughty words coat the pages, including words that can sound aggressive and negative. If such language may upset you, this is not the book for you.

MORE THAN JUST A VERBS THESAURUS

This book is more than just a verbs thesaurus. Much more. It's a learning tool for writing and editing your sexy scenes, a sex-scene planner, and contains inspiring additions.

How would you like to learn how to spice up your sex scenes?

You can, with this *Voluptuous Verbs* thesaurus!

At the end of this volume, you'll find several appendices for your learning and brainstorm pleasure.

- Appendix A: A Tip, Just the Tip - Internal Thoughts
  - What she's thinking and what he's feeling during the act
- Appendix B: How to Write a Good Sex Scene
  - The six components to making it steam off the page
- Appendix C: Sex Scene Planner
  - Templates and ideas to plan your spicy scenes

- Appendix D: Find and Fix
  - Editing your scene to clean it up, making it nice and wet
- Appendix E: Liz's Favorites — Verbs
  - My favorite verbs from this thesaurus

These additions are inspired by my writing method. I hope they help. Have fun with them and adapt them to your own creative process!

VOLUPTUOUS VERBS: HOW TO USE THIS BOOK

While just incorporating strong verbs in your story can improve the quality of your writing, to make the sec scene even spicier, as I mentioned in the previous section, I've included a bunch of writing tools in the appendices.

Of course, feel free to use this book as a simple thesaurus. See what works for you. Find the fun to get the writing done!

Because examples help, here is one suggested process for using this book:

1. Read the appendices A through C at the end of this book on how to write a sex scene. These sections address: the growth of the inner selves, the relationship, the inner consequences, the outer consequences, the subtext, the wild card, and internal thoughts.
2. As you write your story and arrive at a sex scene, first answer the questions in "Appendix C: Sex Scene Planner Template" to get clarity on the purpose of the scene.
3. Complete the full first draft of your story.

4. Then edit it enough so that it feels close to a final draft.
5. Go to a sex scene.
6. Use this thesaurus to strengthen the verbs. The verbs are organized from the early stages of desire to the big O and after-cuddles. I recommend you write down the verbs you like most in the "Personal Favorites" section in the back of the paperback version or underline the verbs in the ebook version.
7. Lastly, use "Appendix D: Find and Fix" as a guide to finesse the quality of the writing throughout your story.

If this method doesn't work for you, come up with your own and have fun with it!

INTRODUCTION TO VOLUPTUOUS VERBS

Early in his career, Steve Martin joked, claiming he wrote and published many, many brilliant novels. When he mentioned the release of his book, *The Apple Pie Hubbub,* he said, "The Apple Pie Hubbub was a significant novel for me, because that's when I first started using verbs."

As funny as his comment was, strong verbs are critical to storytelling. That said, I plead guilty to using "was" a lot.

Some of my favorite authors captured my heart because they used strong verbs, verbs that replace "was" with words the reader can feel in her gut and bones, verbs that steer the protagonist's story through treacherous waters. Your goal with your story is to capture the reader with your vivid and compelling prose and never let her go.

Some writers may think that bedroom romp scenes can feel predictable because there's a limited amount of verbs that work for those kinds of scenes. But that feeling of predictability begs the question, "How can an author make this sex scene unlike any other scene their readers have read before?"

One way is to use powerful, visceral verbs.

WHAT ARE VERBS? AND HOW CAN I MAKE THEM YUMMY?

The Merriam-Webster dictionary defines a verb as a word that shows an action (lick), an occurrence (harden), or a state of being (was). State of being verbs typically connect non-verbs together to reveal more about a person, place, or object.

For example: The sauna **was** hot. The gentleman inside **was** naked. By the looks of him down there, he **was** happy to see me.

OVERVIEW OF HOW VOLUPTUOUS VERBS IS ORGANIZED

I've organized the chapters of this book in the order an act of physical intimacy might happen: From admiring each other to wanting each other, to removing clothes, to touching and kissing, to tasting and growing aroused, to making love and cuddling.

Note: Some verbs are listed multiple times in different categories because they have different connotations.

A WORD ON GENDER LANGUAGE

When I describe a relationship in this book, for the purposes of clarity and convenience, the protagonist is female, and the protagonist's partner is male. These descriptions can be applied to LGBTQ+ scenes by changing the pronouns.

This is the book I wanted on hand when writing my spicy scenes. I hope it comes in handy for you, too.

VOLUPTUOUS VERBS

LOOK

Quickly:

Flicker
Glance
Glimpse
Scan
Skim
Sparkle
Spot
Twinkle

Subtly:

Cloak
Conceal
Mask
Peek
Peer
Scout
Shield
Shroud

Spy
Veil

Obviously:

Gape
Gawk
Ogle
Stare
Watch

Continually:

Admire
Appraise
Beam
Behold
Drag
Focus
Gaze
Haul
Observe
Perceive
Pore over
Peruse
Regard
Study
View

Curiously:

Examine
Explore
Eyeball

Gander
Inspect
Scrutinize
Snoop
Survey

WANT

Slightly:

Admire
Fancy
Have an inclination for
Hanker
Pine
Yen for

Strongly:

Ache
Burn
Covet
Crave
Desire
Hunger
Itch
Long
Lust
Need

Require
Salivate
Thirst
Want
Wish
Yearn

REMOVING CLOTHES

Remove Clothes:

Expose
Free
Liberate
Release
Rip off
Show
Strip
Tear off

Lift skirt:

Hike up
Hitch
Raise

Undo:

Unbind

Unbuckle
Unfasten
Unlace
Untie
Unstrap

TOUCH / KISS

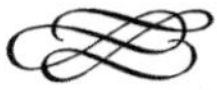

Barely:

- Blow
- Breathe
- Drift
- Encounter
- Feather
- Flirt
- Float
- Glide
- Graze
- Hover
- Kiss
- Pause
- Peck
- Skim
- Surf
- Trace
- Trail
- Whisper

Gently:

Aggravate
Annoy
Brush
Compress
Creep
Doodle
Exasperate
Glide
Knead
Madden
Massage
Palm
Plague
Press
Prowl
Rub
Ruffle
Shadow
Skulk
Slink
Slither
Sneak
Stroke
Sweep
Tantalize
Tease
Tempt
Trail
Toy
Vex

Lovingly:

Attuned to
Bestow
Captivate
Caress
Cherish
Composed
Concentrate
Constrict
Draft
Enchant
Flutter
Frolic
Indulge
Inscribe
Jot
Knead
Massage
Pacify
Pat
Pet
Pleasure
Prance
Press
Romp
Scribble
Squeeze
Squish
Strum
Thrill
Thrum

Curiously:

Amble
Analyze
Breach
Catalogue
Consider
Dawdle
Evaluate
Explore
Fiddle with
Gauge
Linger
Map
Meander
Meditate
Ponder
Press on
Probe
Prod
Question
Reflect
Request
Roam
Rove
Scheme
Scout
Sneak
Speculate
Spy
Squeeze
Steal
Stroll
Toy
Traipse

Urge
Wander
Wiggle
Wriggle

Thoroughly:

Cross-examine
Drug
Dwell
Excite
Exhume
Explore
Finger
Fixate
Fondle
Handle
Hypnotize
Indulge
Interlace
Know
Lace
Lavish
Mesmerize
Mine
Obsess
Pace
Partake
Pleasure
Ravish
Roam
Rove
Spread
Stimulate

Treat
Unearth
Validate
Venture
Wake
Wiggle
Wriggle

Aggressively:

Ambush
Assail
Blitz
Bombard
Charge
Claim
Clasp
Clutch
Fasten
Fidget
Glean
Grasp
Grill
Grip
Grope
Harvest
Hoard
Imprint
Interrogate
Jerk
Knead
March
Nab
Own

Palm
Parade
Paw
Pluck
Possess
Press
Pull
Ravish
Reap
Rub
Rush
Scamper
Scramble
Scurry
Secure
Seize
Snatch
Squeeze
Stitch
Storm
Stroke
Tether
Trot
Tug
Wring
Yank

Mouth/Kiss:

Affix
Bind
Bestow
Delve
Fasten

- Glue (his mouth to hers)
- Indulge
- Kiss
- Partake
- Pin
- Press
- Seal (his mouth to hers)
- Secure
- Sneak
- Steal
- Strap
- Trace
- Tongue

Vagina:

- Breach
- Cup
- Deepen
- Delve
- Electrify
- Excite
- Fill
- Finger
- Fist
- Fit
- Indulge
- Infuse
- Instill
- Kiss
- Massage
- Masturbate
- Poke
- Probe

Prod
Rub
Seize
Sink
Stimulate
Stir
Stretch
Stroke
Submerse
Test
Tempt
Thrust
Tongue
Toy
Venture
Wake
Wiggle
Wriggle

Penis or Clit:

Blow
Caress
Clasp
Clench
Clutch
Embrace
Enchant
Encounter
Enfold
Engulf
Excite
Fist
Kiss

Grab
Grasp
Grip
Indulge
Jerk
Massage
Masturbate
Polish
Press
Pull
Sculpt
Seize
Stimulate
Squeeze
Stroke
Tempt
Tongue
Toy
Trace
Tug
Wake
Wrap
Yank

Nipple:

Clasp
Clutch
Electrify
Enchant
Encounter
Excite
Flick
Grab

Grasp
Grip
Kiss
Nab
Palm
Pinch
Pluck
Press
Pull
Roll
Seize
Snag
Squeeze
Stimulate
Tempt
Tongue
Toy
Trace
Wake

Breast / Buttocks:

Amass
Capture
Caress
Clasp
Clench
Clutch
Collect
Cradle
Cup
Engulf
Grab
Grasp

Grip
Grope
Kiss
Knead
Massage
Nab
Pluck
Press
Sculpt
Seize
Snag
Squeeze
Toy

ATTACK

Attacking:

- Ambush
- Anchor
- Assail
- Assault
- Attack
- Blitz
- Bombard
- Bound
- Charge
- Drive
- Hold down
- Jump
- Leap
- Lunge
- Overcome
- Pin
- Pluck her rose
- Pounce
- Ravish

Rush
Seize
Startle
Storm
Throw himself upon
Wrestle

SURPRISE

Surprise:

Amaze
Astonish
Astound
Daze
Dazzle
Floor
Resist
Shock
Startle
Stun
Stupefy
Thrill

EAT

Greedily:

- Chow down
- Cram
- Devour
- Gobble
- Gorge
- Gulp
- Indulge
- Polish off
- Ravish
- Wolf

A large amount:

- Dine
- Feast
- Indulge
- Lunch
- Overindulge
- Sup

A small amount:

Munch
Nibble
Partake
Snack
Taste

Hesitantly:

Choke down
Peck at
Pick at

DRINK

Daintily:

Partake
Sip

Noisily:

Carouse
Slurp

Greedily:

Drain
Guzzle
Indulge
Knock back
Swallow
Swill

SUCK

Sucking:

- Devour
- Encircle
- Encompass
- Enfold
- Engulf
- Envelop
- Nurse
- Ravish
- Savor
- Suck
- Swallow
- Take in
- Wrap (their mouth)

LICK

Licking:

- Circle
- Dance
- Flick
- Glaze
- Lap
- Lave
- Lavish
- Lick
- Snake
- Slurp
- Swirl
- Taste
- Tease
- Test
- Titillate
- Tongue
- Trace
- Twirl

BITE

Daintily:
- Nibble
- Tease

Continually:
- Chew
- Gnash
- Gnaw
- Munch

Quickly:
- Nip

GROW (NIPPLES AND GENITALS)

Bigger:

Arise
Billow
Blossom
Bud
Bulge
Distend
Elongate
Flex
Flower
Fortify
Grow
Harden
Inflate
Jut
Lengthen
Mushroom
Protrude
Puff
Pump

Rise
Stiffen
Stir
Stretch
Swell

AROUSE

In the early stages:

Arouse
Awaken
Beckon
Bolster
Bud
Commence
Disquiet
Elevate
Entertain
Entice
Evoke
Excite
Fan
Kindle
Ignite
Incite
Inflame
Intoxicate
Itch

Palpitate
Percolate
Pique
Provoke
Raise
Reel
Ruffle
Salivate
Scintillate
Shake
Shudder
Smolder
Spurred
Stew
Stimulate
Stir
Stress
Tantalize
Tempt
Thrill
Tingle
Titillate
Transcend
Tremble
Wake

In an exquisitely bad way:

Ache
Agitate
Agonize
Beguile
Boil
Bother

Brew
Burn
Charm
Consume
Enchant
Enrapture
Fan
Madden
Plague
Race
Roast
Scorch
Simmer
Stoke
Throb
Torment
Torture
Vex
Yearn

Hard:

Excite
Flaunt
Flex
Menace
Pebble
Stand
Stiffen
Jut
Threaten
Tighten
Wag

Wet:

Celebrate
Drench
Dribble
Drip
Drizzle
Drool
Enjoy
Excite
Flow
Froth
Lavish
Liquefy
Moisten
Ooze
Pool
Puddle
Rain
Saturate
Seep
Shower
Soak
Spill
Splash
Trickle
Well

Nearing Climax:

Corkscrew
Crank
Creep
Revolve
Rotate

Spin
Tickle
Twirl
Madden
Wind

GET INTO POSITION

Bend Back:

- Arc
- Arch
- Curve
- Flex
- Stiffen

Bending Over:

- Bow
- Hunch
- Stoop

Onto Knees:

- Buckle
- Crouch
- Kneel
- Sink

Lie Down:

Lean back
Lie back
Lie down
Recline
Repose
Sprawl

Give In:

Acquiesce
Assent
Assume
Cave
Comply
Consent
Embrace (her situation)
Entertain
Lend (herself)
Open
Relent
Resign
Submit
Surrender
Yield

PENETRATE

Deeply:

Anchor
Bore
Burrow
Bury
Clog
Cram
Crunch
Deepen
Delve
Drill
Exhume
Explore
Fasten
Fill
Fit
Imbed
Imprint
Indulge

Infuse
Inject
Inscribe
Know
Load
Lock
Lodge
Lunge
Mend
Mine
Pack
Park
Plant
Pledge
Plunge to the hilt
Probe
Restore
Seal
Secure
Sink
Slip
Stuff
Submerse
Tunnel
Unearth
Wade

Forcefully:

Afflict
Ambush
Assail
Assault

Besiege
Blitz
Bombard
Bore hard
Brand
Carve
Charge
Claim
Cleave
Cram
Cross-examine
Drive
Endure
Enjoy
Exert (himself)
Force
Gore
Grill
Hack
Halve
Have
Impale
Interrogate
Intrude
Invade
Jab
Lance
Mince
Overcome
Overindulge
Own
Pierce
Pilfer

Pluck her rose
Possess
Run
Rush
Saw
Shred
Slice
Spear
Split
Stampede
Startle
Sting
Stamp
Stomp
Storm
Stuff
Subject to his blows
Surge
Take possession
Trample
Vandalize
Vaporize

Hard:

Accelerate
Advance
Astonish
Astound
Bewilder
Blaze
Bombard
Boost

Bound
Bulldoze
Bump
Celebrate
Challenge
Churn
Collide
Confront
Crash
Dash
Daze
Dazzle
Driving home
Enjoy
Entertain
Fly
Frolic
Hammer
Hasten
Heave
Hike up
Hoist
Hurry
Hustle
Jackhammer
Jam
Jog
Jolt
Jostle
Labor
March
Muscle
Pace (himself)
Parade

Partake
Pave
Plod
Pluck her rose
Plunge
Polish off
Pound
Prance
Press
Prod
Propel
Pummel
Punch
Race
Raise
Ram
Ravish
Ricochet
Romp
Scamper
Scorch
Scramble
Screw
Scurry
Shock
Shove
Shuffle
Slam
Slap
Smack
Smite
Sock
Spank
Speed

Sprint
Strain
Stretch
Stride
Strike
Strive
Stroke
Strum
Strut
Stuff
Stun
Swagger
Sweep
Take pleasure in
Throttle
Thrust
Thump
Toil
Trot
Vault

Gently:

Adjust
Aggravate
Alter
Amend
Angle
Annoy
Arrest
Attune to
Breach
Confound
Control (himself)

Corrupt
Creep
Curb
Customize
Dawdle
Delay
Delve
Deposit
Deviate
Dip
Diverge
Drift
Ease
Edge
Enter
Glide
Guide
Gyrate
Halt
Hide
Hinder
Incline
Inch
Insert
Instill
Irritate
Jut
Linger
Lumber
Lurk
Madden
Maintain (a rhythm)
Meander
Modify

Mosey
Mystify
Negotiate
Nudge
Pace
Pause
Peck at
Pivot
Place
Plague
Poke
Postpone
Press
Probe
Prod
Prowl
Push
Question
Refine
Restrain
Revise
Request
Resist (burying himself in one quick thrust)
Restrain (himself)
Roam
Saunter
Savor
Set
Shift
Sink
Skulk
Slide
Slink
Slip

- Slither
- Snack
- Sneak
- Squelch
- Stall
- Stay
- Steal
- Stick
- Stir
- Stroll
- Suppress
- Suspend
- Swivel
- Tailor
- Taste
- Test
- Thrill
- Thrum
- Torment
- Torture
- Traipse
- Treat
- Twist
- Validate
- Venture
- Vex
- Wake
- Wander

In and Out:

- Back and forth
- Gyrate
- Hammer

In and out
Jackhammer
Pummel
Shuttle
Stroke

BEING PENETRATED

Giving in:

Accommodate
Acquiesce
Bow
Buckle
Cave
Release
Relent
Relinquish
Resign
Submit
Succumb
Surrender
Yield

Vagina Grip:

Acquiesce
Accommodate
Cave

Celebrate
Clasp
Clench
Clutch
Comply
Compress
Constrict
Embrace
Endure
Enfold
Engulf
Entertain
Grasp
Grip
Mold
Relent
Resign
Seal
Seize
Sheath
Squeeze
Submit
Surrender
Wrap
Yield

COUPLING

As a Couple:

Attach
Blend
Combine
Connect
Consummate
Couple
Fuse
Join
Merge
Mold
Rendezvous
Share
Unite

BREATHE

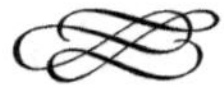

Heavily:

Gasp
Heave
Hyperventilate
Pant
Rasp
Sigh
Suck
Wheeze

In short burst:

Blow
Puff

SOUNDS

Sounds:

- Bang
- Bop
- Crack
- Glug
- Slap
- Slosh
- Slurp
- Smack
- Squeak
- Thump
- Thunk
- Thwack
- Whack
- Whomp

MOVE

Get in Position:

Anticipate
Pose
Positioned
Prepare
Ready (herself)

With Arousal:

Gyrate
Melt
Ride
Squirm
Tremble
Undulate

From Sex:

Jerk
Jiggle

Quiver
Waggle
Wiggle
Wriggle

In Delicious Agony:

Arch
Claw
Contort
Curl
Flail
Quiver
Squirm
Stiffen
Struggle
Thrash
Tremble
Twist
Writhe

ORGASM / CLIMAX

In Tiny Pieces:

Crumble
Crush
Shatter
Smash

In Large Pieces:

Crack
Fracture
Fragment
Snap
Splinter

Beyond Repair:

Atomize
Disintegrate
Melt
Pulverize

Ruin
Wreck

Explosively:

Burst
Bust
Explode
Flatten
Gush
Level
Obliterate
Pop
Rupture
Rush out
Spend
Spill

Off a High Place:

Capsize
Cascade
Descend
Drop
Keel
Nosedive
Overturn
Plummet
Plunge
Rain
Reel
Spiral
Swoon
Topple

Tumble
Upend

Fly Gently:

Glide
Soar
Float
Fly
Hover
Levitate
Ride
Transcend

Granted To:

Appease
Award
Compel
Deliver
Divested
Induce
Present
Provoke
Reward
Share

Giving In:

Accommodate
Acquiesce
Bow
Buckle
Cave

Release
Relent
Relinquish
Resign
Submit
Succumb
Surrender
Yield

Violent Movements:

Bunch
Clench
Clutch
Compress
Constrict
Contort
Convulse
Flex
Grapple
Jerk
Quake
Scuffle
Seize
Shudder
Skirmish
Struggle
Thrash
Tremble
Tremor
Tussle
Twitch
Twist
Undulate

Wrangle
Wrestle

Movements Afterward:

Palpitate
Pulse
Pulsate
Quiver
Rock
Shiver
Shudder
Throb
Tremble
Vibrate
Waver
Wobble

After Orgasm:

Abate
Assuage
Cease
Diffuse
Diminish
Ease
Ebb
Extinguished
Fade
Fizzle
Hush
Mollify
Muzzle
Pacify

Purr
Quell
Recede
Reel
Satiate
Satisfy
Subdue
Throb
Wane

VOCALIZE

Softly:

Beckon
Beg
Beseech
Cajole
Choke
Chuckle
Coax
Coo
Entreat
Giggle
Groan
Growl
Gurgle
Heave
Hiss
Hum
Implore
Invite
Mew

Moan
Murmur
Pacify
Pant
Plea
Plead
Purr
Rasp
Sigh
Sniffle
Snivel
Sob
Snuffle
Sputter
Stammer
Stutter
Utter
Wheeze
Whimper
Whisper

Loudly:

Bawl
Bay
Bellow
Break down
Cheer
Command
Croon
Cry
Egg on
Exclaim
Holler

Howl
Inspire
Keen
Lament
Laugh
Proclaim
Rave
Roar
Scream
Screech
Shout
Shriek
Spur
Squeal
Wail
Weep
Yell
Yowl

Short Tones:

Bark
Gasp
Grunt
Gulp
Huff
Puff
Yelp
Yip

EJACULATE

Throw:

Blow
Cast
Chuck
Discharge
Eject
Expel
Flick
Fling
Heave
Hurl
Infuse
Inject
Instill
Jet
Jettison
Let fly
Load
Pitch
Rain

Release
Run
Shoot
Sling
Soak
Spill
Spout
Spray
Sprout
Spread
Spurt
Squirt
Stream
Toss
Vandalize
Vaporize

Release:

Acquiesce
Award
Bestow
Cave
Complete
Contribute
Deface
Deliver
Deposit
Dispense
Drench
Dump
Eject
End
Enrich

Exude
Feed
Fill
Finish
Flood
Flow
Gush
Inundate
Jet
Lavish
Nourish
Outpour
Overflow
Present
Provide
Release
Relent
Relinquish
Resign
Reward
Ricochet
Saturate
Share
Seed
Slosh
Soak
Spend
Splash
Spurt
Submit
Surrender
Swamp
Yield

After Orgasm:

- Bubble
- Dribble
- Drip
- Drizzle
- Drool
- Glisten
- Ooze
- Pool
- Puddle
- Seep
- Spill
- Throb
- Trickle

EMBRACE

Before Penetration:

- Bed
- Capture
- Climb
- Embrace
- Ensnare
- Entangle
- Entwine
- Hold
- Hug
- Lay (beside)
- Merge
- Mount
- Position
- Recline
- Rendezvous
- Seize
- Snare
- Straddle

In One's Arms:

Bundle
Collapse
Embrace
Encircle
Encompass
Enfold
Engulf
Envelop
Hug
Lock together
Mold
Unite
Wrap arms around each other

Afterward Lovingly:

Assuage
Bed
Cherish
Connect
Cuddle
Ease
Embrace
Entwine
Hold
Hug
Laze
Nestle
Nuzzle
Pacify
Relax
Renew

Snuggle
Soothe

APPENDIX A: A TIP, JUST THE TIP - INTERNAL BELIEFS

APPENDIX A: A TIP, JUST THE TIP - INTERNAL BELIEFS

MOTIVATION IS KEY: KNOW WHY ONE PERSON LOVES THE OTHER

It's important to be clear on why the protagonist loves or at least wants to have sex with her companion.

Why?

Because knowing why she loves her partner clarifies to the reader: a) what kind of person the protagonist is attracted to, b) what beliefs the protagonist needs to hold to get along with her partner, and c) in what way the partner assists (or prevents) the protagonist with (or from) achieving her goals.

Use these following questions to uncover your protagonist's motivations for loving their partner.

What kind of people is your protagonist attracted to? How does she explain the attraction to herself?

What beliefs does her partner have regarding family, sex, spirituality, money, and other aspects of his day-to-day life? Are these beliefs part of the attraction? If so, in what way? Be specific.

THE PROTAGONIST'S TRANSFORMATION ARC AND GOALS

Does the protagonist currently share the same beliefs as her partner, or will we see how the relationship will reshape her and change her beliefs?

Do her partner's beliefs help her or hinder her with advancing toward her personal goal?

What are some other ways her partner helps or hinders her with reaching her goal?

A PRESENT FACT, A TRUTH

On occasion, I've read sex scenes where the protagonist comes to a conclusion about courting behaviors, gender roles, cosmic influence, etc. Chloe Thurlow does a good job of this.

The idea is as follows. Just before or while starting the act of sex, there may be time for the protagonist to reflect. This is a moment when she's not purely focused on reaching climax. Instead, she can notice how she feels in the moment. She may feel more confident than expected when obeying a stranger's command to undress, taking off her bra in front of him. Her conclusion may be that women are blessed with beauty and may not realize it until others gaze upon them like a work of art.

Whether or not this "truth" is actually true or not doesn't matter. What matters is what the protagonist believes and how it will further her path to become the person she needs to be by the end of the book.

What are some "facts" or "truths" the character needs to believe to have what she wants at the end of the story? How will having such beliefs help her become the person she needs to be?

APPENDIX B: HOW TO WRITE A GOOD SEX SCENE

CONTENTS OF APPENDIX B

INTRODUCTION: HOW TO WRITE A GOOD SEX SCENE

When it comes to writing romance, the layers of the sex scene make the scene meaningful. There are at least four layers to consider. One layer is to pinpoint how the sexual interaction will change the protagonist's inner self. Another layer is to consider how the sex will change the relationship between the two lovers. Two more layers are about the inner and outer consequences of becoming so intimate.

Those four considerations — the inner growth, the growth of the relationship, the inner consequences, and the outer consequences — are a good minimum amount of layers to place in a sex scene.

There are two other layers I invite you to consider.

The fifth layer: What is the subtext of the scene? That is, what secrets are the lovers keeping during this moment of vulnerability?

The sixth layer: What is the unique situation or environment, the wild card that makes this sexual act different from almost every other sex scene you've written or read?

I love that last one and strive for the wild card as much as I can!

When it comes to erotica, keep in mind that the moment of change in the character arc of the story, the "Point of No Return" in the Hero's Journey story structure, is often not sexual in nature. But the consequences of the moment of change will be most noticeable the next time the lovers have sex.

HOW WILL THEIR INNER SELVES GROW?

In nearly every story, a character changes internally in some meaningful way. Often, the character knows what kind of person they wish to become — strong, independent, loved, or confident — and the character pursues that goal. Good writing shows the character growing incrementally toward that goal and achieving it. Better writing shows the character growing incrementally toward that goal, then becoming someone else, someone unexpected, fulfilling an internal goal she didn't even know she had.

When it comes to sex scenes, consider what happens during the act that changes the character. What is that one incremental piece of growth she achieves because of each sexual bout?

Maybe she has insecurities about her nakedness and a loving man gave her the wisdom to challenge those insecurities. Maybe all she knows how to do is give and a loving partner who gives her oral pleasure helps her start to see the value in receiving. Notice I used the words like "challenge" and "start." The idea is not that her lovers heal her, but that they help her gain the strength to confront her inner demons herself.

The intimacy doesn't always have to lead to growth in the right direction; she may have put all her eggs in one basket and, at the end of the scene, something about the act has completely destroyed her original plans.

The idea is that the reader feels all is lost for the protagonist, and the protagonist is not only right back where she started, but often in a worse place than when she started. The difference is that she has grown incrementally so much throughout the story leading up to this point, that she now has the inner tools to overcome such an obstacle. Also, overcoming this huge obstacle will greatly contribute to helping her become the person she needs to be to have her happily ever after if you're writing that kind of story.

So, when writing a sex scene, consider what it is about her, internally (her beliefs, her sense of self, etc.), that will change by the end of the scene.

HOW WILL THEIR RELATIONSHIP GROW?

In romance fiction, the moment when the relationship has crossed the first threshold where ignoring the attraction is no longer an option is often called "The Point of No Return." This point occurs roughly a fourth of the way into the story, and that's a very loose estimate. The moment can occur much sooner or much later, but the point is it occurs in Act 1 of the story.

This romantic point of no return in romance is when a character does something in the budding relationship between the two protagonists that has changes their relationship so much, there's no way to restore the way it was, even if they wanted to. The action could be a dance, a kiss, sex, or simply realizing they really, *really* like each other. Once that happens, they must spend the rest of the story figuring out what should take priority, their love for each other or their lifelong goal, be it their job or their pursuit of wealth or any other life goal. But in romance, love always wins.

In erotica, however, the sex act is not unique enough to be the action that represents the point of no return. More often, there needs to be something different about the emotional connection between the two that represents the point of no return.

For example, if an actor and actress work at an X-rated theater and every night perform a sexual act for the audience, their relationship may be one of friendship and just making a living. The point of no return might be the moment when the actress gains a boyfriend, and the sexual actor finds he's more jealous than he thought he'd be. Or perhaps the actress needs some emergency financial assistance and, after meeting at a restaurant with the actor to ask for his help, he agrees and from then on she feels the sexual act with the actor is more intimate than before.

In the first example, the loss of full sexual attention triggers the change in their relationship. In the second example, having a vulnerable discussion over a medium-rare steak and a Waldorf salad brings the two closer together.

To put it another way, in erotica, it's not the physical act that changes the relationship, it's the change in intimacy that brings them to a point of no return. Once that point of no return has passed, then consider what will be different when they have sex again. Will the thrusts be gentler? More aggressive? Will they be noticing the other's expressions more? Will they demonstrate more concern over how the other is feeling?

For your protagonists after the point of no return, have fun with inventing ways their relationship and interactions will be different for them.

WHAT ARE THEIR INNER CONSEQUENCES?

In romance, the budding relationship deals with the potential consequences of sex.

Your protagonist will have questions.

Will having sex with him now ruin my feelings of friendship with him?

Will I regret this in the morning?

Will I feel like a slut afterward?

You can certainly have her feel like a slut or feel like she lost a friend after the sex act, but hopefully the protagonist gains something positive from the experience, too.

What does she gain? Better self-confidence? An appreciation for her fantasies? A bigger desire to take care of others?

If you're challenged by determining what your protagonist gains from the sexual act, consider her overall inner goal. How will the physical intimacy help nudge her closer to becoming the kind of person she wishes to become?

In erotica, however, it's not the sex act that raises such questions; perhaps she often has sex with this partner. It's the moment of intimacy that carries important consequences.

Questions your character might ask herself:

Will having a new boyfriend disrupt my professional relationship with my stage sex partner?

Will having dinner with my stage sex partner change our relationship in ways that could ruin our professionalism?

As a consequence of intimacy, have fun exploring the opportunities to create positive consequences for how your main character views herself.

WHAT ARE THEIR OUTER CONSEQUENCES?

Just as budding relationships involve questions about inner consequences, they also involve questions of outer ones.

Your character might ask:

Will having sex with this person ruin the friendship?

Will he later lose respect for me?

Will he become so obsessed with me that I'll later discover he's psycho?

Though these concerns are similar to the inner ones a character asks herself, the difference is that often problems between the two do come up afterward.

Does having sex with him ruin their relationship? Absolutely!

Does he seem to lose respect for her for being "easy?" You bet!

Is he psycho? Maybe some of the things he does seems strange, and she should have checked his background more closely.

It's these new problems of interacting that are the frequent conflicts which occur in romance.

Unlike outer consequences, the inner consequences are

ones which any smart, empowered character can take control over. Readers prefer smart, empowered characters.

Outer consequences, on the other hand, are out of the character's control. She can't control how her partner feels, or what they say or do. And since good stories require challenging obstacles to overcome, the conflicts between her partner and herself are good obstacles to use. It won't matter how smart or empowered she is, she can't snap her fingers and change how he feels about her or behaves toward her. (Although, that could be a good story!)

All those changes in feelings and behaviors because of sexual encounters are standard in romance.

In erotica, however, it's those moments of verbal intimacy and vulnerability separate from sex that generate the outer consequences.

As an example, I once read an erotic story of a man who always hired the same prostitute and had her play a schoolgirl in bed. To his surprise, it turned out she was, indeed, a college student and, in a moment of opening her heart to him, she was desperate to borrow money from him to pay her tuition. He gladly helped her out, but the next time she came over as a schoolgirl for roleplay, he was unable to get an erection. That moment of realizing she was truly a schoolgirl ruined the fantasy for him.

What about your protagonist? Uncover the challenges she has after intimacy when interacting with others. Have fun with it!

WHAT'S THE SUBTEXT?

The subtext in a story is the unspoken underlying situation in the scene. Most of the time, that subtext evolves from the secrets the characters keep from each other.

Fortuitously, one of the most powerful pieces of storytelling is secrets. They keep the stakes high and the reader turning pages. The reader wants the secret revealed.

There are three main types of secrets. Brainstorm all three types for your protagonist, so you can create a powerful subtext in your sex scenes and keep your reader deeply engaged.

SECRETS THE PROTAGONIST KEEPS FROM OTHERS

During sex, what is the secret the protagonist is keeping from the partner?

For example:

Is she having sex with him to make his brother jealous?

Is she having sex with him to get closer to his boss, the CEO of Peach Music Incorporated?

Imagine the protagonist has just been fired from her job and her husband has been relying on her salary to pursue his dreams. She might come home, undo his trousers, ritually stimulate him into full arousal, and think about nothing but how his erection looks.

It can be heartbreaking to read about a woman who ought to be thinking sad thoughts over losing her job but instead is ignoring her sadness. It can be heartbreaking to notice that not only is she avoiding telling her husband about losing her job, but she is working hard to put the harsh reality out of her own mind.

Writing this type of scene—what she's not revealing to her husband, and seemingly suppressing from her own experience—is what creates subtext. That which is inferred by the reader but not shown on the page.

SECRETS THE READER KNOWS, BUT THE PROTAGONIST DOESN'T KNOW

What is the secret the reader knows that the protagonist doesn't?

For example:

Does the reader know that the protagonist's sex partner is secretly married?

Does the reader know that the sex partner is secretly a shape-shifting demon posing as the protagonist's boyfriend?

To write this kind of secret into the scene, the reader needs to know the secret beforehand.

SECRETS THE PROTAGONIST KNOWS BUT THE READER AND OTHER CHARACTERS DON'T

What about a secret the protagonist is keeping from both her lover and the reader?

These are the most fun and perhaps the hardest to write.

For example, before she enters her boyfriend's apartment building, she scans the street and sidewalks, makes sure no one is around, then takes out a piece of paper and writes something on it and nearly gets caught by her boyfriend.

What was she writing? Why was it necessary to hide it from her boyfriend? I have no idea! Argh! But it makes for compelling reading because maybe there will be some other odd things she does during her snog with her boyfriend that will reveal what she's hiding.

That's subtext! Ultimately, when writing a sex scene, you can add another layer by considering what secret is being kept, by whom, and how.

Enjoy creating subtext on the page to keep your readers intrigued, wanting to know more, and turning the pages to find out.

THE WILD CARD

I love the wild card.

Adding a wild card is about making your particular sex scene unlike nearly any other sex scene.

Readers expect that most every sex scene will involve two (or more) partners becoming physically intimate with their attention focused on either giving or receiving an orgasm or accomplishing both.

What if you added something unrelated into the mix?

As a kind of game, think of a random object or a task unrelated to the upcoming romp of pleasure and see if you can incorporate it in your scene.

For example, in my *Goldie's Locks and the Three Men* story, Goldie poses as a call girl and joins her client at a private room in a casino hotel. When they debate over who should get serviced first, they decide to flip for it. Throughout the scene, they rely on a coin, heads or tails, to see what to do next in bed. Here, I used a game of chance to literally create an unexpected environment for the protagonists and to keep the readers guessing.

As another example, in my *Alice's Salacious Adventures,*

Lessons from Wonderland book, Alice meets a young man who has never seen a woman before. So, to her delight, he goes exploring. Later, she meets his friends who have also not seen a woman before and, when she suggests there may be a prize inside her, they take turns trying to find and taste it.

To simplify the process of coming up with wild card in the scene, consider who the protagonist's lover is. What are his unique skills or flaws? Maybe he's a wizard who has lost his powers of making things disappear. She can help him by encouraging him to make her dress disappear, then her bra, then her panties. Just the motivation he needed to recover his powers!

Maybe he's a professional whistler at music studios and he finds just the right frequency that gets her to climax. Things could get interesting when she denies her heart's longing to be with the whistler because she has to have dinner with her mean fiancé and her fiancé's parents. It could be that while she suffers through the conversation at the restaurant, the whistler sits at a nearby table and whistles her special frequency, making her a hot mess in front of her fiancé and soon-to-be in-laws.

You can also consider the wildcard to be elements of the environment. Maybe she's a stowaway on a flight to London and accidentally hides in the same spot as another stowaway. The hiding place is cramped and hot. Very hot. Taking off their clothes is just their way to survive the temperature, but when the plane experiences turbulence, their bodies grow with inconvenient need.

By adding this wild card layer to the sex scene, you are not only adding to the growth of the character and moving the story forward, but you are also providing the reader with new ideas for fantasies with your creativity. Have a lot of fun with this one!

APPENDIX C: SEX SCENE PLANNER

CONTENTS OF APPENDIX C

INTRODUCTION

As you write your story, you might arrive at a perfect spot for your protagonist and her beloved to engage in advancing their intimacy by interlocking limbs. But suppose you're concerned that the scene will not be meaningful to advancing the story and the relationship.

The template for this sex scene planner can help you address that concern by focusing on these ten topics, all explained in the previous sections of Appendix A and Appendix B:

- Reasons why she loves him (and vice versa)
- Possible concerns each one has
- Ways their inner selves will grow from the physical experience
- Ways their relationship grow from the experience
- Some inner consequences of having sex
- Some outer consequences of their physical intimacy
- Possible subtext

- How the act will transform the protagonist
- Possible wild cards
- Possible "facts" or "truths" she concludes during the experience

TEMPLATE

Determine what will occur in the sex scene:

1. Why do they love each other? Why are they attracted to each other?

2. What are the possible concerns each one has? (Choose ones that are different from the inner and outer consequences.)

3. How will their inner selves grow?

4. How will their relationship grow?

5. What are the inner consequences?

6. What are the outer consequences?

7. What is the subtext?

8. Knowing what *you* desire the protagonist's transformation to be, what must the quality of the sexual interaction be like?

- The Protagonist's Transformation:

- Sex:

9. What is the wild card, (I.e. sex by dice, environment, secret voyeur, etc.)?

10. What is a present-tense "fact" or "truth" the narrator acknowledges or discovers during sex?

IDEAS

If you're short on ideas for your planning, I've offered suggestions here to spark your imagination.

Reasons why she loves him (and vice versa):

He takes care of her emotional needs, financial needs, or physical needs.

He supports her goals and dreams.

He understands her quirks and kinks.

He accepts and admires her weaknesses.

He helps her complete tasks and chores she cannot do alone.

He needs her emotionally, financially, or physically.

He treats her the way she expects to be treated, which could be positive or negative.

He's gorgeous.

He thinks she's gorgeous.

Possible concerns (choose one that will be different from her inner and outer consequence):

They will take their friendship to a more intimate level.
She'll get pregnant. He'll want the baby, too.
She'll get pregnant. He won't want the baby.
He'll think she's ugly naked.
He'll only want a one-night stand.
They'll end their friendship.

Ways her inner self will grow from having sex:

Boosts her confidence.
She feels needed.
She feels admired.
She feels desirable.
Diminishes her confidence.
She feels expendable.
She feels humiliated.
She feels ugly.

Ways the relationship will grow from having sex:

They trust each other more.
They desire each other more.
They communicate better.
They do everything together.
They spend some more time together.
One wants to spend more time with the other, but the other doesn't want to.
They struggle with communicating.
One stalks the other.
Trust is broken.
They never want to see each other again.

Hidden traits are revealed and now they no longer desire each other.

Some inner consequences of having sex:

She gains confidence.
She trusts herself more.
She admires herself.
She loses confidence.
She can no longer trust herself to do the right thing.
She despises herself.

Some outer consequences of having sex:

They take their friendship to a more intimate level.
Her parents encourage her to get married to him.
She gets pregnant. He wants the baby, too.
She gets pregnant. He doesn't want the baby.
They end their friendship.
If it was an affair, she breaks up with her husband.
She gets cut off from her girlfriends.
She gets cut off from society.

Possible subtext for the sex:

"He thinks I'm agreeing to a one-night stand, but I love him."

"I only want his baby."

"I only want his wealth."

"This is revenge sex with my boyfriend's best friend."

"I want this sex to be a story I can brag about to my girlfriends."

"This affair is my passive-aggressive way of making my

fiancé break up with me, so cancelling the wedding won't be my fault."

"I have herpes and want to spread it to as many dumb, mean guys as possible."

Ways the quality of the sex can lead to the kind of outcome or transformation you want the protagonist to experience. Think of the transformation the protagonist will have, then determine the kind of sex that will lead to that transformation:

- **The Protagonist's Transformation:** She expects a one-night stand but falls in love.
- **Sex:** She experiences gentle lovemaking when she's so used to men using her to get their rocks off.

- **The Protagonist's Transformation:** She ends up trusting him.
- **Sex:** He coaxes her to close her eyes and surprises her with great lovemaking.

- **The Protagonist's Transformation:** She ends up no longer trusting anyone.
- **Sex:** He's her closest friend and, while blindfolded, he treats her as a toy to use. When he takes off her blindfold, she sees she's surrounded by his frat brothers and roommates who laugh at her and call her a slut.

Possible wild cards:

Props: ropes, blindfolds, dildos, strapons, etc.

Creative props: puppets, conscious items like salacious bed covers, flipping a coin to see who gets served, living water in a swimming pool, a dildo that grows when pedestrians talk to her, etc.

Settings: Private (i.e., bedroom), secret (i.e., under the table at a dinner party), public (i.e., on the baseball field during the World Series).

Strange lovers: a third partner, an orc, a dragon, the living wind, the living sun, etc.

Possible "facts" or "truths" she concludes during sex: These so-called facts may not be true, but the reader should be able to believe that the character would come to such conclusions due to her experiences.

"Men think they're the powerful ones when they're physically on top, but they're so out of control with desire, they don't realize that women are the ones in power."

"There's nothing more humiliating than two women tied face to face. And nothing more exciting."

"When men use the right words, women want to obey them."

"Men are obsessed with breasts. They're content with doing no more than ogling them."

"Throughout history, women were forced to cover up with modesty while wearing clothing that exuded sex, training men to desire the sight of a naked woman. He was no exception."

EXAMPLE

Below is a sample scene I wrote using the *Appendix C: Sex Scene Planner Template*. Notice that the scene advances the heroine's character arc, the hero's character arc, the relationship's arc, and, in this case, generates complications.

Why do they love each other? Moycie loves him for helping her get her Heavenly Bites dessert catering business started. Kent loves her for being not only human—one who can be open to improving his personal code of ethics—but also because she has demonstrated a growth mindset willing to be open to all things strange, including having a relationship with a wizard.

Possible concerns?

Concern Before Sex: Moycie is worried that Kent will break up with her, but instead, she has to be comfortable not trusting her reality when he's around.

How will their inner selves grow? Moycie will feel comfortable being unable to discern reality when Kent's around. Kent feels trusted and appreciated for his magic.

How will their relationship grow? They become a couple.

What are the inner consequences? She finds a beloved who commits to supporting her crazy entrepreneurship dream.

What are the outer consequences? She has someone who will actively help her goal of running a dessert catering business. Kent has been disowned by the entire Wizard community.

What is the subtext? Her experience isn't real.

Knowing the transformation or outcome you want the protagonist to have from the scene, what must the quality of the sexual interaction be like?

- **The Protagonist's Transformation:** Moycie learns Kent's secret and embraces it.
- **Sex:** Wildly magical.

What is the wild card? The ring is Kent's connection to being with other wizards, the environment isn't real, Moycie has sex with a water creature.

What is Moycie's fact? Men will agree to anything when you have their cock in your hand.

Moycie paced in her living room and straightened the cooking magazines on the oakwood coffee table.

Kent would be here any minute. There was "something important" he needed to tell her? Was he going to stop dating her? Was there another woman?

She sat on the cream-colored couch and exhaled.

Relax, Moys. The way his gaze often lingered on her cleavage and long legs, he's been wanting to plow her ever since they first started dating three months ago. Her body was willing and eager to satisfy his desire. And if he did indeed plan to stop dating her, changing his mind would be a breeze. All she had to do was grip his aroused cock, put it close to her lips, and tease him until he said the magic words: "I want you to be my girlfriend." Good plan.

The doorbell rang. She jumped to her feet.

Time to shine.

She checked that the collar of her sherbet orange blouse was straight. She smoothed out any wrinkles in her tan, bootcut pants and hastened to the door.

He smiled with that mesmerizing grin framed by dimples. "Hey, Moys."

She kissed his cheek. He didn't resist. Good sign.

"Did the business licensing department call you?" he asked.

"They did. What a relief. I don't know how you convinced them to approve my license, but thank you."

"You're worth it. And after tasting your cupcakes, the whole county deserves to also enjoy that pleasure."

An image of Kent holding her breasts for guests at a party to taste them flashed through her mind. Her face burned hot.

"You okay, Moys? Your face turned red."

"Fine." She giggled and fanned herself. She gestured to the couch, but he sauntered to the matching armchair and tugged on the knees of his navy blue suit trousers as he sat. "Can I get you anything, Kent? Coffee? Tea?"

He shook his head. "Before we go any further in this relationship, there's something you need to know."

Before going further? He didn't want to screw her first and then unveil the bad news? That could ruin her plan of convincing him to be her boyfriend, teasing him with his hard flesh in her fist.

"You sure you don't want to tell me later?"

He motioned to the couch for her to sit.

Oh, well. So much for her plan.

She sat across from him, the coffee table between them.

"Ever since I met you, I've admired your openness to try new things." He loosened his topaz tie and ran a hand through his scruff of auburn hair. "I don't know how to tell you this, so I'm just going to come out and say it."

She stiffened.

He twisted the ring with the ruby jewel on his finger, the one he inherited from his family.

Here it comes. Another good man lost.

He inhaled, then exhaled. "I'm a Mind Wizard."

She blinked. "Uh… what?"

"I can do what you humans often refer to as Jedi mind tricks."

"You humans?"

"Yeah. You know how I said my parents and my sister live in Birmingham? They actually don't live in the U.S."

"You lied to me?"

"Not exactly. They live in Birmingham, England. Not Birmingham, Alabama. And, well, they're wizards, too."

She shook her head. "Is this some passive-aggressive way to stop dating me? You can tell the truth. You can tell me you're not into me. I'm a big girl."

"No!" He leaned forward. "I *am* into you. It's just..."

He fiddled with his ring again.

"Just what, Kent?"

"I'm a Mind Wizard."

She threw her hands in the air, stood and paced. "For Heaven's sake. Here I was, ready to... ready to go to bed with you, and you come here with some story about being a Jedi that can do magical powers. How am I supposed to respond to that?"

His jaw dropped. "Ready to do what now?"

"Prove it. Prove to me you're a wizard."

"You planned on sleeping together?"

"Yes, now prove it. Show me your magical mind tricks."

He bit his lip, then said, "How do you like the beach?"

Seagulls squawked overhead. Moycie spotted them flying above her in a clear blue sky. What the—? To her side, gentle waves of the ocean splashed along the shore. The rhythm of the waves calmed her.

"Your cellphone's ringing."

Dizziness claimed her head. She paused to steady herself. Her phone called out to her with another ring. She stepped to her tote bag that rested on a boulder and retrieved her vibrating phone.

"Hello?"

"It's me," Kent said. "How do you like the beach?"

"It's gorgeous." There was something off. Something obvious. But she remembered planning this trip and driving all the way to the ocean. What could be off? She breathed in the salty sea air. "I wish you could be here with me."

"How does the sand feel?"

"Just a sec." She kicked off her shoes, removed her socks, and wiggled her toes in the sand. "The sand is hot."

She walked closer to the waves where the sand was cooler.

"It's hot there?"

The sun heated her skin with delicious rays. "Very."

"Is anyone around?"

She looked left and right. "I'm alone."

"Is there a breeze?"

A light breeze caressed her. "Yes."

"Set your phone down, Moys. Put me on speaker and take off your clothes."

"Good idea."

She returned to the hot, dry sand. After setting the phone on the sand safely away from the waves, she ambled back to the cooler sand, closer to the water.

She unbuttoned her orange blouse, the sunlight spreading more and more across her chest. She slid the sleeves off her arms and let the blouse float to the ground. She reached back and unclasped her bra, freeing her breasts. The bra fell. She erased the sweat from under her breasts, then squeezed away the memories of their confinement.

A kind breeze gave her relief.

She plucked open the snap of her tan pants and unzipped them. With one movement, she yanked her pants and panties down her legs. Her breasts jiggled as she bent over and freed her legs.

"Are you naked, Moys?" Kent's voice asked from her speakerphone. His voice sounded tinny and a little faint since the phone was a few feet behind her, away from the wet sand.

"Yep. Feels great." She lay back on the cool sand and

closed her eyes. Her breasts, belly, and legs soaked in the sunlight.

"What do you feel now?"

"The waves that come to shore spread across my feet and calves. Oh!"

"What happened?"

"A bigger wave came all the way to my hips. There! It did it again." Her pussy tingled from the splash. "Every few waves, the wave is big enough to reach my waist."

"How does it feel."

She giggled. "I like it."

A few more waves came and went, stimulating her. She caressed the sides of her torso and grazed her skin with her fingertips. Her nipples pebbled. She cupped them.

"Open your eyes, Moys. There's a water being in front of you."

She gasped at the sight of a man-shaped creature made of water. He focused on her naked body. She could almost see through the being, but his form was clear. The swirling eyes, the tongue that licked his lips, the broad shoulders, the muscles in his arms, and yes, the giant erection that demanded attention.

"Please." She backed away in a crab walk on her elbows and feet. "Don't hurt me."

"Don't worry, Moys. Water beings never hurt people."

"But it looks like he's going to..."

"Don't worry, Moys. He can't do anything without your consent. Try touching him."

Was Kent crazy? Yet, the water being made no move toward her. She inched closer to him and, when she was close enough, she raised her hand close to his chest.

He didn't flinch and he didn't attack.

She touch his chest. Her fingertips went through as if

touching a waterfall. His pouring chest flowed around her fingers. His erection still looked solid, though.

"Try touching it," Kent said.

"His dick?"

"Trust me, Moys. You're safe."

She gently touched his tip with a finger. The finger went through like it had his chest.

"Squeeze it, Moys," Kent said.

Squeeze it? She wrapped her hand around his length. With a soft touch, her fingers started slipping through. But when she tried closing her fist, he became firm. And bigger.

"What do you notice, Moys?"

"The harder I squeeze him, the more solid he becomes."

"And if he were inside you?"

Whoa! If he entered her, all she'd have to do is clench and he'd grow harder, thicker, and bigger.

"Lie down, Moys. Enjoys yourself."

Hell, if Kent was willing…

She lay back and closed her eyes. The water creature slipped inside her. The cool temperature made her clench. Wow! Harder. Thicker. Bigger. A rush of heat raced through her core, across her legs, along her chest, and sparked her nipples.

The water creature flowed through her entrance, filling her more and more, delighting her with cool comfort as the sun prickled her skin. Every few waves, a bigger wave splashed across her, joining the fun between her thighs.

"How do you feel, Moys?"

She gasped and caught her breath. "Incredible."

The giant thrust faster, and her heart pounded. She used her free hand to clutch a breast. Pleasure rippled across her chest. Heat traveled up her shoulders and neck. Her pussy tightened around the being's enormous length, and she shook with an orgasm that clenched the muscles in her legs and toes, curled her torso, clamped the hand on her breast, and she cried out to all that was joy and abundance and decadence.

The water creature splashed out of her and washed away, taking her essence with him into the ocean.

Her delightful spasm passed, but a few jolts and shivers of pleasure lingered.

"How do you feel, Moys?" Kent said.

"Satiated." She panted.

"I'm going to release you from the spell. You'll see that you're not at the beach. You're on the rug of your house. I'm sitting over you. Naked."

What was he talking about?

But the sky darkened. A ceiling was overhead. There was no more sound of seagulls or ocean waves. Kent sat naked on his knees beside her, his arousal quite large and unfinished. His hand was between her thighs, two fingers buried inside her, keeping still, calming her from the strong climax she had. The ruby of his ring applied a delicate pressure against her clit.

She glanced around the room. Yep. Her house. No beach.

"You really are a wizard."

"I am. About the beach and the water being. I'm sorry if I deceived you with a false—"

She grabbed hold of his length and pumped him. He moaned.

"Come closer to my mouth," she said. Her renewed excitement made it hard to keep steady breaths.

He shifted closer and swung a knee to the other side of her head. Her head was sandwiched between his thighs.

She stroked him. "You want me as your babygirl?"

He wavered, struggling to sit upright.

"Say it. Tell me you want me to be your girlfriend."

"Of course," he puffed. "That's what I wanted ever since I met you."

She pulled him into her mouth and sucked and licked and slurped.

"Yes!" He responded by maneuvering his fingers inside her.

Damn, that ring felt great on her clit.

He released jet after jet down her throat. It tasted minty, not salty. Did he use his mind tricks to make her think it tasted good? Did it matter?

She grabbed hold of his butt cheeks and pushed him deeper into her mouth, lapping at every drop she could get with the lingering question of whether playing a trick on her mattered or not.

It really didn't.

When he was finished and she could find no more minty flavor on him to lick, he collapsed at her side. She cuddled into him, and they lay there, naked, on the shaggy rug of her home.

Something seared her back. "Ow!"

He jerked his hand off her. The ring was glowing hot. Then disappeared from his finger.

"What happened?" she said.

"It's the tradition of Wizards. When we commit to a human, we're disowned by our families."

"What does that mean?"

"My parents, my sister, all my friends I grew up with have sensed our coupling. I can never see them again."

"But that's crazy. Can't you go to England and talk to them about it?"

He shook his head. "They want nothing to do with me now."

Unbelievable. Everyone needs their family. "It makes no

sense for you to sacrifice your past just to be with me, so… Maybe us being together? Maybe that's not a good idea."

He propped himself on his elbow, "No, Moys. The past is over. You're my future. You're my woman. And I'm your man."

He kissed her, sealing the promise of their future together.

What comes next? Does Moycie confront Kent's family to convince them to accept her? Does Kent's sister hate losing Kent and try to kill Moycie? Was there another woman, a wizard, who was promised to Kent in an arranged marriage?

Feel free to reprint this scene and write a full story around it. Write your Moys and Kent story, upload it to online bookstores, and make some money. No need to ask for permission! All I require is that the subtitle be **Moys and Kent** (See what I did there with what it sounds like? I'm naughty.), so that I can easily find your creative spin on the story when I do a search on the bookstore's search engine.

APPENDIX D: FIND AND FIX

APPENDIX D: FIND AND FIX

Recently, I was inspired by Cara Bristol's book, *Naughty Words for Nice Writers,* to add this additional "Find and Fix" appendix, because she has a section titled, "Naughty Words to Avoid," which lists weak words to eliminate so that one can tighten the quality of their writing.

Just like my "Find and Replace" Appendix in my *Naughty Nouns in Historical Romance* in the *Thesaurus for Romance Authors* series, where I provide a simple way to make the writing sound more historic, I provide this similar "Find and Fix" Appendix to improve one's quality of writing based off my own writing process.

I encourage you to purchase Cara Bristol's *Naughty Words for Nice Writers* as an additional invaluable addition to your writer's resources shelves. One of the things Bristol's book includes that my books do not is a detailed thesaurus for spanking scenes.

DEEPER POV

Make the protagonist's point of view deeper (deep POV) to help the reader relate to the protagonist. The writer's guide *Deep Point of View* by Alice Gaines is a wonderful resource for more clarity on what deep POV is, when to use it, and how to use it effectively.

CUT:

- She thought that
- She felt that
- She considered
- She planned
- She wondered
- She heard
- She saw
- She smelled

Replace with what you might say in your own head, like, "The deep V of his tunic beckoned her hands to explore underneath. Mmm."

TIGHTEN SENTENCES

Tighten sentences by eliminating unnecessary words. If the meaning of the sentence changes when the word is removed, it's okay to keep the word for clarity.

CUT:

- Began to
- Started to

- Tried to
- Was increasingly becoming
- Just
- Seemed to
- Very / so

ADVERBS

Eliminate all adverbs that end with -ly because constantly, endlessly, and persistently reading words that end in -ly can distract the reader. You can replace the verb-adverb combination with one stronger verb. "He squeezed her breasts tightly" could become, "He seized her breasts," or "He gripped her breasts," or "He clenched her breasts."

PASSIVE VOICE

Avoid passive voice and flip the subject and object of the verb to make the voice more active. For example, "she was grabbed by him and was pulled into an embrace" is not only a lot of extra words to read but also makes the characters sound weak and without agency. Instead, write: "He grabbed her and pulled her into an embrace."

TO BE OR NOT TO BE

Avoid "was" as a verb and replace it with stronger verbs. When using "was" to describe something like a person's features or clothes, or the weather or surroundings, replace the sentence by starting with the item to describe and how it affects one of the characters.

For example, instead of, "It was a hot day," write, "The scorching sun soaked the undersides of her breasts with sweat revealing two wet smiles side by side on her white Tshirt." We can infer it was a hot day by that sentence. I like Cara Bristol's rule of thumb: limit yourself to about an average of three uses of "was" per page.

MEANWHILE...

A pet peeve of mine is the use of "as" and "while" in sex scenes. Instead of, "He lavished her clit with licks as he slid a finger inside her while she moaned," use "and" or start a new sentence, like, "He lavished her clit with licks and slid a finger inside her. She moaned."

PRONOUNS

Stick to using only "he" or "she" or any non-binary pronouns instead of using the name, especially of the character who holds the POV. Saying the names over and over can remove the reader from the relatability of the character, distancing us from the character. The best time to use names are when it's necessary to clarify who's talking or which character the prose is talking about.

FULL EXAMPLE

All of these tips can help improve your writing. Read the following before and after example to see how these tips can improve and tighten your writing.

A rough draft of a naughty scene might look like this.

Before

Alice thought that the deputy was fingering the widow under the interrogation room table. Over the widow's face was a black veil, so it was hard to see the widow's expression. Alice wondered whether the reason the widow remained still was because the widow was too shocked to push away a man with a badge. The deputy's behavior was insufferable. Alice felt that all deputies wanted to have their way with female suspects and prisoners. Alice planned to have a word with the police sergeant about the deputy's behavior.

In the interrogation room, Alice heard the widow's breaths starting to become increasingly labored. A moan was stifled. Alice saw the widow stoop over the table. The woman began to move uncontrollably with subtle, tiny orgasms. Alice felt her nipples tingle. A part of Alice considered that, as much as Alice was against the deputy's behavior, the pleasure the deputy seemed to have the widow experience was just so very hot to watch. Alice wanted to pull off the widow's veil quickly and see if the widow's eyes were rolling to the back of the widow's head as the widow's nostrils flared while the widow bit her lip.

Here's a more polished version, using the find and fix method:

AFTER

The room wafted with tart arousal. Was the deputy fingering the widow under the interrogation room table? The black veil obscured the widow's face. Perhaps the woman remained still because she was too shocked to push away a man with a badge. He was getting away with it. Unbelievable. His brazen behavior was no surprise, though. All deputies wanted to have their way with female suspects and prisoners. A word with the police sergeant about this inappropriate behavior should put a squeeze on the deputy's scrotum.

In the interrogation room, the widow's breaths became labored and she stifled a moan. The woman in mourning clothes stooped over the table and shook with subtle, tiny orgasms. Alice's nipples tingled. As much as she despised the deputy's behavior, the widow's inhibited release of pleasure made Alice's heart pound. What if she snatched the widow's veil to expose her face? Would the widow's eyes be rolling to the back of her head, nostrils flared? Would she be biting her lip?

EXERCISE

Find a few paragraphs from your work in progress, copy and paste them into a new document, then apply these tips to your writing. What worked? What didn't work?

Don't worry about writing first drafts in pristine form. Pausing too often in your writing process can slow your production, leading to analysis paralysis. Instead, for your first draft, write crap.

To use these tips, punch the "Find" command in the document to search for such problem spots as using the extraneous words "thought," "felt," "began," "just," etc, and fix your writing.

You got this!

APPENDIX E: LIZ'S FAVORITES — VERBS

APPENDIX E: LIZ'S FAVORITES — VERBS

Below are my favorite verbs to use in a sex scene. They delight me in many sinful ways. You can use this list as an inspiration to create your own. In the print edition, I've added a blank page for you to jot down your favorites.

Sex (From early years to recent years):

Swiving
Fucking
Pleasuring
Stroking
Doing
Frigging
Poking
Shagging
Mounting
Riding
Laying
Screwing

Masturbation (From early years to recent years):

Frig
Rub
Toss off
Milk himself
Jerk off
Rub one off
Diddle
Finger
Finger-fuck
Jack off
Jill off

Penetrate

Deeply:

Anchor
Burrow
Bury
Delve
Fill
Imbed
Load
Lodge
Pack
Sink
Stuff
Submerse
Tunnel

Forcefully:

Cram
Impale
Jab

Pierce
Storm
Stuff

Hard:
Blaze
Bombard
Crash
Drive home
Hammer
Jam
Plunge
Pound
Pummel
Ram
Ravish
Shove
Slam
Thrust

Gently:
Breach
Delve
Ease
Enter
Glide
Guide
Insert
Nudge
Press
Probe
Push
Savor
Sink

Slip
Test
Venture

Vagina Grip:

Accommodate
Clasp
Clench
Clutch
Constrict
Embrace
Enfold
Engulf
Grasp
Grip
Mold
Seize
Sheath
Squeeze
Wrap

Give In:

Accommodate
Acquiesce
Cave
Relent
Resign
Submit
Surrender
Yield

Orgasm:

Come
Spend
Melt
Get there
Cream
Get off

Female:

Burst
Bust
Clench
Clutch
Constrict
Contort
Convulse
Crack
Crumble
Disintegrate
Fracture
Fragment
Gush
Jerk
Melt
Plummet
Plunge
Quake
Rupture
Shatter
Soar
Spill
Spiral
Splinter

Thrash
Topple
Tremble
Tumble
Twitch

Male Ejaculate:

Award
Deliver
Drench
Eject
Enrich
Fill
Flood
Infuse
Inundate
Jettison
Lavish
Release
Reward
Saturate
Seed
Shoot
Soak
Spend
Spray
Spurt
Squirt

After Orgasm:

Dribble
Drip

Ebb
Fade
Ooze
Purr
Reel
Satiate
Seep
Throb
Trickle
Wane

Cry out / Vocalize

Softly:
Coo
Groan
Hum
Moan
Purr
Sigh
Whimper

Loudly:
Bay
Cry
Howl
Screech
Wail
Yelp

YOUR PERSONAL FAVORITES - PRINT EDITION ONLY

Note here which verbs are your favorites so that you don't need to keep flipping through the pages.

AUTHOR'S NOTE

I hope this has been, and will often be, a helpful resource for you.

Having written so much erotica (20 books and counting!), I thought this *Thesaurus for Romance Writers* series would be a great venue to drip some of my favorite writing techniques. And I hope that by the end, I wasn't the only one dripping. 😊

Please let me know if there are sections and terms you uncovered that are missing from these books so that I may update them. You can email me at LizAdams-Books@gmail.com and put THESAURUS WORDS in all-caps in the subject line so that I don't accidentally miss your email.

Also, check out the other books in this series if you want more synonym help: *Arousing Adjectives* and *Naughty Nouns in Historical Fiction*.

And hey! I encourage you to try all the exercises and templates in this series. Every master starts a disaster. The way to master your writing is by drafting and editing and getting feedback on your writing, over and over.

The good news is that writing sex scenes is fun!

As my friend and author Chloe Adler once said in describing the process of writing erotica, "You write some, then go to bed. Write some more, then go to bed. Write some more, then go to bed." Your readers will get the benefit of reading your steamy scenes in bed without having to alternate.

For all you readers of saucy tales, if you're interested in discovering which sexy superhero you are, take my quiz at http://www.LizAdamsAuthor.com. You can also join my reader community and get a free short story about what Wonder Woman's sex life might be like!

UNLOCK THE SECRETS TO WRITING IRRESISTIBLE SEX SCENES

Discover the Perfect Words to Elevate Your Romantic Scenes

This *Thesaurus for Romance Writers* series comprises of three passionate volumes dripping to satisfy your needs, each designed to elevate your writing and make your love scenes steamy:

1. Voluptuous Verbs (this book)

Why settle for mundane descriptions like "she took off his pants" when you can spice things up. Replace it with, "She unbuckled, unzipped, and unsteadied him." Find verbs that penetrate your scenes and leave your readers panting. This thesaurus includes writing tips on how to use the bedroom scene to develop the heroine's inner growth, her inner and outer consequences, the relationship's consequences, the subtext of the scene, and the wild card.

2. Arousing Adjectives

While overusing adjectives in regular scenes is a faux pas, they are indispensable when the clothes come off and the lovemaking begins. Dive into words that paint vivid pictures, like "sprouting, thick, eager, hot, frenzied, throbbing, strong," for him, and "supple, taut, pluckable, quivering, tangy, velvety, wet," for her. These adjectives will transform your spicy scenes into scenes your readers will read again and again. Included in this thesaurus are exercise on how to write at different heat levels, and how to incorporate the character's goal, motivation, conflict, and stakes in your delectable, lip-smacking scenes.

3. Naughty Nouns

A perfect resource for historical romance writers! This book of synonyms is your go-to guide to determine whether grabbing hold of his "length" fits the time period of your Regency romance. Which terms did they use back then? Discover the historically accurate terms that set the mood just right. This thesaurus includes tips on how to use explicit words to incite excitement instead of sounding like an anatomical textbook.

A Must-Have Resource for Every Romance Writer

Whether you're crafting a steamy Regency romance or a contemporary love story, use the books in the *Thesaurus for Romance Writers* series — invaluable resources that will help you find the perfect words to set hearts racing and pulses pounding in your spicy scenes with captivating synonyms. It has been a game-changer for me, and I hope it will be for you too.

ACKNOWLEDGMENTS

I started the *Thesaurus for Romance Writers* series when historical author and friend Regina Kammer guided me and other authors to Jonathon Green's outstanding online interactive timeline of sexy terms and their first moments of popular use. The timeline focused on historical synonyms for genitalia and intercourse. From there, I launched into other sources, ones which provided synonyms for words not addressed by the timeline. Most of the new terms came from a standard thesaurus. Then, I added terms not originally meant to be sexy. For example, synonyms for "breaking apart into pieces" were terms I categorized under Climax.

Over the years of using my private thesaurus, the list of words became longer. And, oh, so much longer. Historical erotica like *The Autobiography of a Flea* and *My Secret Life: An Erotic Diary of Victorian London,* and a few short lists of sensual terms elsewhere, I added more words to the mix.

That done, I studied the layouts of other romance Thesaurus books—including ones by Cara Bristol, Valerie Howard, and Stefanie Olsen—and determined the layout I thought was most useful.

Lastly, my brilliant writing coach Beth Barany helped me with edits and ways to market this series.

The inviting covers were designed by 100 Covers, and I appreciate all the hard work they put into the design.

And thank you, dear writer. The world needs your stories. *I* need your stories. Keep writing!

~Liz

ABOUT THE AUTHOR

Award-winning author of best-selling spicy, paranormal fairytales, Liz Adams tires her hands at the keyboard spinning steamy, surrealistic fantasies — some historical, some contemporary, some futuristic — so that her readers can also tire out their hands until the happy endings. She loves leaving her readers breathless and soaked.

Want to know a secret? Playing loud music while reading might hide your squeals of delight. Just sayin'.

She lives in the gorgeous San Francisco Bay Area, and in her spare time, she enjoys movies on the couch cuddling with her spouse and two cats.

If you enjoyed this book, please write a review!

Liz would love to know how you heard about her ebook, so drop her a line at LizAdamsBooks@gmail.com or at her website:

http://www.LizAdamsAuthor.com.

She's always eager to connect with her readers and would love to hear from you.

MORE BOOKS BY WRITER'S FUN ZONE PUBLISHING

Overcome Writer's Block: A Self-Guided Creative Writing Class to Get You Writing Again

(Writer's Fun Zone Book 1)

The Writer's Adventure Guide: 12 Stages to Writing Your Book for Novelists and Creative Nonfiction Writers

(Writer's Fun Zone Book 2)

Twitter for Authors: Social Media Book Marketing Strategies for Shy Writers

(Writer's Fun Zone Book 3)

Plan Your Novel Like a Pro: And Have Fun Doing It!

(Writer's Fun Zone Book 4)

7 Essential Keys to Planning Your Novel: Story Preparation for Pantsers

(Writer's Fun Zone Book 5)

Mastering Deep Point of View: Simple Steps to Make Your Stories Irresistible to Your Readers

by Alice Gaines

ALSO BY LIZ ADAMS

FAIRY TALE EROTICA

Alice's Salacious Adventures, Lessons From Wonderland

(Adventures of Alice, Book 1)

A titillating two-book collection

Alice's Story of O, Princess and the Pea

(Adventures of Alice, Book 2)

An interactive, spicy fairytale

Alice's Frisky Freaky Friday, Hansel and Gretel

(Adventures of Alice, Book 3)

A body-swapping, dark fairytale

Alice's Snow White and the Seven Sins

(Adventures of Alice, Book 4)

A reverse-harem spicy fairytale

Alice's Labor of Love, Tasting Cinderella

(Adventures of Alice, Book 5)

An intoxicating, oral fairytale

Alice's Study in Little Deaths, Aesop's Fables

(Adventures of Alice, Standalone)

A suspenseful, spicy fairytale

Goldie's Locks and the Three Men

(A Modern Erotic Fairy Tale Fantasy for Women)

What if the only way to find the right man was to instead find the right men?

ARIEL'S SUPER POWER OF LOVE

Ever wonder what Wonder Woman's love life was like?

SHERLOCK; THE CASEBOOK OF A SALACIOUS SLEUTH

(4 Spicy Romantic Short Stories)

Feeding his carnal appetite one case at a time.

DE SADE & GRIMM; A SPICY COLLECTION OF DARK DELIGHTS

(4 Supernatural Short Stories)

Can you resist the pleasure when evil claims you?

THE ORIGIN OF TINKERBELL

(A Modern Erotic Fairy Tale Fantasy for Women)

Time stops for the playful.

MAID MARY AND ROBIN HOOD'S MERRY MEN

(A Dark Romance)

A mask can hide you from yourself.

What if your beloved paralyzed you and removed your mask?

SHORT STORIES

AMY "RED" RIDING'S HOOD

(Fairy Tale Erotica)

Would you submit to the beast within him?

BREAKING FREE

(A Kidnapping Romance)

When society suppresses your femininity and your kidnapper encourages it, how can you hate him?

Alina Said, Call Me Maybe

(A Short Romance)

How far would you go, letting a stranger caress you in public?

Sherlock; The Case of the Ripped Bodice

(A Spicy Romantic Short Story #1)

Your client fears he may be Jack the Ripper? Terrific.

Sherlock; The Case of the Invisible Lover

(A Spicy Romantic Short Story #2)

Who haunts her bed?

Sherlock; The Case of Sinbad's Seduction

(A Spicy Romantic Short Story #3)

What will you do when a night of vengeful passion leads to a perilous mystery?

Sherlock; The Case of the Voyeuristic Vampire

(A Spicy Romantic Short Story #4)

His penetrating gaze awakens your desires.

de Sade and Grimm; An Enchantment of Leaves

(A Dark Supernatural Short Story #1)

What if an unholy fiend unleashed your darkest desires?

de Sade and Grimm; A Seduction of Clay

(A Dark Supernatural Short Story #2)

You awake. No memory. The Clay Master claims he is your husband. Will you yield?

de Sade and Grimm; An Ambush of Cream

(A Dark Supernatural Short Story #3)

How can she fight the invisible, hedonistic foe?

de Sade and Grimm; A Menace of Silk

(A Dark Supernatural Short Story #4)

What invisible force is hell-bent on claiming her?

SHORT STORIES IN ANTHOLOGIES

"The Artist" in Sensexual: A Unique Anthology 2013 Vol 1

If you were a succubus and spotted his morning growth, what would you do?

www.ingramcontent.com/pod-product-compliance
Lightning Source LLC
La Vergne TN
LVHW010100110826
845155LV00028B/419
* 9 7 8 1 9 4 4 8 4 1 7 0 6 *